# Q-IN-LAW

PETER DAVID

Abridged and adapted by Joanne Suter

**GLOBE FEARON**
EDUCATIONAL PUBLISHER
PARAMUS, NEW JERSEY

*Paramount Publishing*

Globe Fearon Educational Publisher, a division of Paramount Publishing, 240 Frisch Court, Paramus, New Jersey 07652. No part of this book may be reproduced or transmitted in any form or by any means, electrical or mechanical, including photocopying, recording, or by any information storage and retrieval system, without permission in writing from the publisher.

Printed in the United States of America
1 2 3 4 5 6 7 8 9 10 99 98 97 96 95 94

ISBN: 0-835-91105-5

**GLOBE FEARON**
EDUCATIONAL PUBLISHER
PARAMUS, NEW JERSEY

*Paramount Publishing*

# CONTENTS

# CHARACTERS

## Crew of the *U.S.S. Enterprise*

**Beverly Crusher**—doctor

**Wesley Crusher**—son of Beverly Crusher; not-yet full ensign on the bridge crew

**Data**—Lieutenant commander and android; serves as the *Enterprise*'s science officer and helmsman

**Guinan**—hostess of the *Enterprise*'s Ten-Forward lounge

**Geordi La Forge**—chief engineer

**Miles O'Brien**—transporter chief

**Jean-Luc Picard**—Captain

**William Riker**—Commander and first officer

**Deanna Troi**—Counselor

**Worf**—Klingon Security Chief

## Other characters

**Lwaxana Troi**—ambassador from Betazed; Deanna Troi's mother

**Q**—very powerful being from the Q Continuum

**Graziunas**—a powerful alien family whose colors are orange and blue

**Nistral**—another powerful alien family whose colors are silver and black

**Kerin**—son of the house of Nistral; betrothed to Sehra

**Sehra**—daughter of the house of Graziunas; betrothed to Kerin

Kerin let out a slow breath. He tried to stop the heavy pounding of his heart. The stars hung around him. These stars had been part of his days for as long as he could remember. He had spent all his 18 years of life in space.

At that moment, he was not thinking about the stars. He was thinking only about the great mother ship of the Graziunas that was huge in front of him. It was dark blue and shaped like a giant egg. Great points of metal stuck out from it at different angles. Smaller ships circled around it, keeping watch for any enemies.

Kerin looked over the controls in front of him as he had done many times before. He knew his high-powered, one-man ship inside and out. It was a gift from his father for his 12th birthday. He remembered his joy the first time he stepped inside the ship. Kerin suddenly noticed his own face mirrored in the viewport before him. He was surprised how much he looked like his father. His hair came to a point on his forehead as was usual for all those of the house of Nistral. His dark eyes were slightly slanted. His skin was a silver color, like polished metal. He had a strong jaw that seemed to say that he knew his own mind.

Now Kerin looked across the controls. His weapons were charged. All engine readings were fine. He had checked everything a hundred times before setting off from the Nistral mother ship. He wanted to be sure of his ship. He would soon have plenty of other things to worry about.

The first of the Graziunas patrol ships had broken off. Two of them were moving closer.

"State your business with Graziunas!" A sharp voice came cutting through the air.

Kerin pushed a button. "This is Kerin of the house of Nistral," he said. "I go where I wish. I do what I wish. I take what I wish."

There was a long silence at the other end.

The answer finally came. "If that is how it must be, then that is how it must be."

Kerin let out his breath. Do it just like you have practiced, he told himself.

He took one more look at the controls. Then he belted himself in and slammed into overdrive.

His ship shot forward. It dipped just under the two fighters. He dropped like a stone and then flew straight toward the great mother ship.

The fighters came after him. Blasts went off on his right and left. Still, his ship moved gracefully through space. "Catch me if you can," he whispered.

A shot hit the right side of his ship. It bumped wildly, but Kerin kept it on course. He shot straight up, but the fighters stayed after him.

"This is your final warning. Turn back with honor." The voice crackled through the air.

"Noted," said Kerin quickly. He slammed the thrusters into reverse.

The fighters shot right past him. They moved into his computer target sights. Kerin opened fire. He clipped the wings of both fighters, stopping them short. This was all he needed. He sailed clear and dove down toward the mother ship.

More fighters were coming toward him now. But Kerin felt more sure of himself as each moment passed. He darted this way and that. Blasts went off around him, but no one was able to pin him down.

The landing bay lay right ahead of him. Suddenly, he was hit. His ship shook. He tried to bring it back under control. He flew wildly into the landing bay. Its walls rushed past him. He was moving too fast. If the nose struck first, the ship would flip over and crash. He would surely be killed. At the last possible second, he edged the nose up. Sparks flew as the bottom of the ship hit the ground. Kerin let out a short yell.

"Hold together, baby," he prayed.

He shut his eyes as he sped toward the wall at the far end. He knew he was going to hit.

The ship half-turned. The back end slammed into the wall. Kerin was forced back against his seat. He gasped as the world spun about him. His ears were ringing from the howl of metal against metal.

Kerin could see the men of Graziunas running toward him. He unbuckled and moved to the door. It would not open. He took out his blaster and blew a hole through the door of his ship.

He jumped out into the landing bay. A guard came at him with a blood-freezing yell, swinging a weapon. Kerin made himself be cool. He fired a quick shot. It hit the guard and knocked the breath out of him. The man lay gasping while Kerin dashed out the nearest door. It hissed shut behind him. He could hear shots landing on the closed door. Kerin wondered if the guards' blasters were on a low setting like his.

The halls of the Graziunas ship were blue and orange. This was quite different from the sharp black and silver that were the colors of Nistral. Kerin looked right and left. He tried to remember which way to go. He had carefully learned the layout of the ship, but now he wasn't so sure. He felt his blood pounding. Then he heard another pounding. It was that of feet close behind him.

He took a right and then another right. Then he took a left and—

He came to a quick stop. The light was so bright! There he stood in the open doorway of the grand chamber of Graziunas.

Graziunas was the name of the house. It was also the name of he who was head of the house. It was a name passed down through the ages.

The present head of the house of Graziunas was a big man with a wide chest. Red hair swept back over his bright blue face. A long red mustache hung down well past his chin.

The great room was crowded. Everyone was standing. Everyone was watching Kerin.

Next to Graziunas stood his daughter, Sehra. Word that Kerin was coming must have reached her. She looked excited and was watching Kerin's every move. She was slim where her father was heavy, but her eyes were as firm and steady as her father's.

Graziunas walked toward Kerin. Kerin stood tall and still, ready to fight. No one spoke. The only sound was the whisper of Graziunas's boots on the floor. His long cape was blue, trimmed with orange. It swirled about him with every step.

Graziunas stopped in front of Kerin. He folded his arms.

"Yes?" he said. His voice was deep and powerful.

There was, however, just a bit of a laugh behind his words.

Kerin's mouth moved. Nothing came out. Graziunas watched him closely. Kerin felt himself growing weaker under his eyes. He looked at Sehra. She was mouthing something, trying to help him.

Finally, Kerin was able to speak. "I come here," he said, "to beg something of thee." He prayed that his voice would not crack. "And I come as one who demands."

"Demands what?" said Graziunas.

"Demands the hand of thy daughter in marriage."

He saw Sehra quickly shake her head with alarm. He knew he had made a mistake. Everything had to be just so. "Demands the hand of thy *most honorable* daughter in marriage," he quickly said.

"What if I do not agree?" asked Graziunas.

Kerin stood taller. "Then I shall fight thee for her. With every breath in my body, I shall fight thee. She shall be mine, and I hers, until all the stars burn away."

Graziunas threw a quick right punch. Kerin quickly ducked. There was a gasp from the people of the court. Kerin came in quickly and swung at Graziunas's face.

Graziunas caught the boy's arm tight.

Kerin grunted. Graziunas's hold was like steel. He

closed his hand tight on the boy's arm. He waited for Kerin to cry out.

But Kerin was the young man who would one day head the house of Nistral. He would not cry out, no matter how sharp the pain. He bit down on his lower lip to stop any sound of weakness.

The room was silent. Everyone was waiting to see if Kerin would make a noise. Nothing. His body was shaking. Blood began to run down his chin.

Graziunas laughed loudly. He let go of Kerin, and the boy fell back a few steps.

"Thou has shown spirit, son of Nistral," said Graziunas. "Thou has spoken the words as they should be spoken. Thou has shown fire." He stepped back and waved toward Sehra. "If she will have thee, then take the hand of my only daughter."

Kerin could not believe it. Smiling now, he crossed quickly to Sehra. She was smiling, too. She held out her arms to him. He took her hands in his.

"You'll have me?" he said, forgetting that he was supposed to speak in the formal manner.

Sehra didn't bother to correct him. "Of course!"

She hugged him tight. Kerin tried not to cry out as she squeezed his sore arm. There were cheers and laughter throughout the room.

"How did I do?" he whispered in her ear.

"Fine." She ran her fingers across his close-cut hair. "You did just fine."

# CHAPTER 2

Guinan did not see Geordi La Forge come into the Ten-Forward lounge. She didn't have to see him, though, to know that he was there.

"Geordi," she said. She glided toward him. Her eyes were bright as the stars outside the viewport.

Geordi looked up at the hostess of Ten-Forward. Or rather, he tipped his head to catch the patterns of her body through his VISOR. There was a coolness about her, an inner calm. He could sense it through the heat waves put out by her body. The VISOR gave Geordi the power to sense things in a different way. He had been blind from birth and often wondered what he'd do if he had a chance to see. It would mean giving up the VISOR and, with it, the powers it gave him. It might be too much to give up.

But today, it was Guinan who was sensing things about Geordi. He was quiet. His usual smile was missing. "Problem?" she asked gently.

"No problem," Geordi answered. But she could see that he had things on his mind.

Guinan went back to the bar and left Geordi to his thoughts. *"I haven't had a serious relationship with a woman in two years,"* he was thinking. *"I can sense a burning coal from 30 feet, but I can't see a woman's eyes burning with love 30 inches away."*

Commander Riker entered. He spotted Geordi sitting alone. Riker walked up and dropped into the chair across from him. "Geordi? Something wrong?"

The chief engineer sighed. "I'm feeling blue."

"You want to tell me about it?" Riker asked. But his communicator beeped before Geordi could answer. He tapped it and said quickly, "Riker here."

"Commander," came the clipped voice of Captain Picard. "To the bridge, please. Bring Mr. La Forge."

"Yes, sir." Riker didn't question how Picard knew that Geordi La Forge was with him.

Jean-Luc Picard rose from his command chair as Riker and La Forge entered the bridge. He nodded toward the meeting room. Worf was already heading there. Riker stopped just short of the door to let the captain enter first.

Picard motioned for Geordi and Worf to go into the meeting room. He held Riker back. "Number One," he said softly, "are you quite all right?"

"I'm fine," said Riker. But he did not seem so.

"You seem a bit put off."

"Just a little down, Captain. It will pass."

At that moment, Deanna Troi entered. "Sorry I'm late, Captain," she said. "I was in a counseling meeting."

Picard nodded. He knew Deanna had important work to do. "The body of a ship runs on the hearts and minds of her crew," said Picard.

"If I may say, sir, you seem unusually happy today," said Troi. She did not need her ability to read feelings to know the captain's mood. He was smiling from ear to ear.

"You will understand why shortly, Counselor."

The captain entered the meeting room. Riker was about to follow. Deanna placed a hand on his arm. "Are you all right, Commander?"

"I don't want to talk about it," he said. He spoke so firmly that she took a step back.

"You just seem a little sad—"

"I'm not sad!" said Riker. Then he marched into the meeting room.

Geordi passed a cup of coffee to Riker and took one for himself. He looked around. Everyone was seated. They were waiting for Captain Picard to begin.

"Gentlemen and ladies," said Picard. He smiled at the group. Dr. Crusher had shown up to join Troi,

Riker, La Forge, Data, and Worf in the meeting room. "We are going to be having a celebration on board the *Enterprise*. We are going to be hosting a wedding for a very important group of people."

"How wonderful!" said Troi.

"Who is it?" said Worf. Unlike Troi's cheery voice, Worf's already sounded worried. Large numbers of visitors on the *Enterprise* meant security problems. Not all members of the Federation were easy to deal with.

"A wedding among the Tizarin," Picard told them. "This is not unusual in and of itself. But this is a cross-marriage between the houses of Nistral and Graziunas."

"I don't get it," said Geordi. "I've never heard of the Tizarin or these 'houses' you are talking about."

Picard looked at Data. "That's your department, Data," he said.

"I will attempt to be short in my reply," the gold-skinned android said. He went on in his calm, almost one-toned voice. "I am beginning to see how a long list of facts can be unwanted in many cases."

"That's very good, Data," Geordi said.

"For example, there was a paper written 37 years ago. Test groups from four races were subjected to 20 hours of information—"

"Data," Picard said quietly. "The Tizarin."

"Oh. Yes. The Tizarin." Data changed subjects without missing a beat. "The Tizarin are a space-going race. They travel about buying and selling goods. If there is a home planet for the Tizarin, it is unknown. They trade with most races in the Federation. They are known to be fair and honest. The Tizarin usually travel in groups of two or more houses. This way they can protect each other." Data went on. "The two houses that the captain named—the Nistral and the Graziunas—are among the oldest and most powerful. These two houses do not always get along. For years, each has tried to outdo the other. But business has been good, and things have been going quite smoothly."

"It has, in fact, turned into something quite promising," Picard said. "The son of the head of the Nistral family has fallen in love with the daughter of the head of the Graziunas family. He has asked for her hand."

"Oh!" said Beverly Crusher, smiling. "How sweet. It's like *Romeo and Juliet.*"

"Ah, yes," said Data. "The play by your William Shakespeare. It deals with angry parents and unhappy teens."

"It was a bit more than that, Data," said Picard. "That play had some of the most beautiful and romantic lines in history. Why, when I was young I was in the cast of *Romeo and Juliet.*"

"Did you play Romeo?" asked Crusher.

"Well, no," said Picard. He suddenly looked as if he wished he hadn't brought up the matter.

"Captain, whom did you play?" asked Riker.

Picard's voice dropped. "I played the nurse."

"The nurse?" said Crusher. "Juliet's nurse?"

"It's a fine part," Picard said.

"Oh, I'm sure you were wonderful, Captain," Dr. Crusher said, smiling.

"In Shakespeare's day, women's parts were always played by men," Picard told them. "*The point is* that in this case the houses are not fighting.The love between these two young people is not a cause for war. It's all been very friendly.

"In fact, Graziunas is quite pleased with the way in which the young Nistral boy asked for his daughter's hand. So you see, Mr. Data, this will not be like the Shakespeare play. There will be no angry parents and unhappy teenagers.

"Now, let us move on," said Picard. "Tizarin weddings are performed by a third party. The Tizarin have asked that the wedding be held on board the Federation's best ship. Starfleet has chosen the *Enterprise*. As captain, I will perform the ceremony.

"We meet with the houses of Graziunas and Nistral in 72 hours. Also, several races who trade with the Tizarin will be sending guests to the wedding."

"I will need a list of those coming aboard," growled Worf. "We must think about security risks."

"My home planet, Betazed, trades with the Tizarin," said Deanna. "The Tizarin do not like to deal with warlike races, Worf. I don't think you need to worry."

"You," said Worf, "can afford not to worry, Counselor. The safety of this ship is my job."

Picard looked at his first officer across the table. The meeting was over. They were alone.

"You seem to have something on your mind, Number One," the captain said.

"Just spring fever," Riker replied.

Picard's communicator beeped. He tapped it.

"Captain," came Worf's deep voice, "we have the information from Starfleet. It lists the guests who will be arriving for the—gathering." He spit out the last word in an angry voice.

Picard turned in his chair to face his computer screen. The names and pictures of important Federation members appeared. The captain nodded as he looked at each listing.

"I have a good feeling about this, Number One," he said. "A celebration like this helps to remind us that love plays an important role in this galaxy."

Picard smiled. But suddenly what he saw made his face turn white.

"Captain, what's wrong?" said Riker.

"Oh, no," said Picard softly. He stared at the screen. "Daughter of the fifth house—"

"Fifth house?" said Riker. Then he understood. "Fifth house of—Betazed."

"Heir to the Holy Rings of Betazed," said Picard in a flat voice. It appears that Deanna's mother will be joining us." Picard groaned. "Lwaxana Troi is being sent by Betazed to the wedding aboard the *U.S.S. Enterprise.*"

"They don't miss a chance to send her off the planet, do they?" Riker wondered.

Picard looked at him. "Would you?"

"Captain, are you all right?"

"A headache, Number One," said Picard. He rubbed the bridge of his nose. "Just a headache. God help us if she's still in phase."

"Yes, sir. Can I get you something?"

Picard turned to the wall behind him. "A cup of tea. Very hot." A small door slid open. A cup came out. Picard took it and sipped. "You have the ship, Number One. I'm going to rest for a few minutes."

# CHAPTER 3

Guinan looked through the viewports of the Ten-Forward lounge. Just outside floated the great ship of the Graziunas family. She knew that on the other side of the *Enterprise* was the house ship of the Nistral. She could see the orange and blue trim that were the colors of the Graziunas. She remembered that the Nistral were silver and black.

Suddenly, Guinan's eyes narrowed. Something was wrong. If she just had a few more moments to—

"This is the Ten-Forward lounge!" came Picard's voice.

Guinan turned around quickly. She pushed aside her worries as the captain entered with four others.

"Guinan," said Picard, "may I present Graziunas and his wife, Fenn? This is Nistral and his wife, Dai. This, ladies and gentleman, is Guinan, hostess of the Ten-Forward lounge."

The guests nodded. The Graziunas, in orange and blue, looked heavy next to the silver and black-dressed Nistral. Nistral was taller and slim, with a beard, but no mustache. He had close-cut black hair and glowing silver skin. Nistral looked as if he was built for hit-and-run type battles.

"Why am I thinking of battles," Guinan wondered.

The wives appeared very much alike. They wore simple, long dresses, each in their family colors. Hoods tied close over their heads gave no hint as to their hair color, or even if they had any hair. It seemed the women wanted to hide anything that might make them special.

"I thought you might like to use the Ten-Forward for the reception," Picard said.

Nistral, who, like Graziunas, was known by the name of his house, looked around the room. "It will do," he said simply.

"How long will you be needing Ten-Forward?" asked Guinan. "How long will the party last?"

"A week," said Nistral quickly.

Together, Picard and Guinan said, "*A week?*"

"Of course, a week!" declared Graziunas. "A week of celebration is quite usual. Are you saying our children are not worthy of that?"

"No, no, not at all," said Picard.

The group turned to leave the lounge. Picard stopped, though, as Guinan called after him.

"Captain, a moment of your time, please?"

He smiled at the Tizarin and made a just-a-minute motion. Then he went over to Guinan.

"Something's up," Guinan whispered in a voice too low for the Tizarin to hear.

"Up?"

"I don't know what it is," she said. "Just a funny feeling that something is going to happen."

Picard had learned to trust Guinan's word. His smile disappeared. "Do you think we should call off the wedding?" He was very sure of her. On her say-so, he would stop the whole affair.

"It will be fine," she said with a calm she didn't feel. "I'll just keep on my toes. If I know more, I'll get to you right away."

Picard nodded. Then he put the smile back on his face. He turned to the Tizarin.

"Now, why don't I show you the bridge."

When the Tizarin had gone back to their own ships, Picard turned to Deanna. "Counselor," he said, "did you get any feelings from them?"

"There is a continuing feeling of conflict, Captain, between the Graziunas and the Nistral. It is well hidden, however, and kept in check. They both want their children to be happy. They have clearly decided to behave themselves."

Picard nodded. "Good. Very good. Putting their children's feelings before their own. Most certainly not a *Romeo and Juliet* situation."

"That is good, Captain," said Data, seriously. "If the bride and the groom were arguing, it would not make for a very merry party."

"Captain," Worf broke in. "We are getting a message from another arriving wedding guest."

Picard remembered which guests were already on board. He had a feeling he knew who was left.

"Put the message on the speaker, Lieutenant Worf," said Picard.

"*Enterprise,*" said a man's voice. "Prepare to transport over the guest from Betazed."

They heard a whisper in the background.

The shuttle pilot added, "A daughter of the fifth house—"

"We'll bring her aboard," sighed Picard. "Bridge to transporter."

"Heir to the Holy Rings of Betazed—" The pilot sounded tired. "*Enterprise,* what is holding things up?"

"Beam her aboard," Picard said.

A moment passed. Then the pilot seemed happier. "*Enterprise,* she is gone. You've got her or you don't. I don't care."

Picard looked quickly at Deanna Troi. She was quite red in the face.

The pilot's voice continued. "I've run a ferry service for Federation members for many years. But I never—that's the last time I take that woman. I'm sorry about her being in mourning, but she never shut up about it the whole trip."

"Mourning!" Deanna's dark eyes grew wider.

Picard turned to Deanna. "Has there been a death in your family, Counselor?"

"I don't know of any, Captain," said Deanna. She rose quickly to her feet.

"Pilot, might I ask for whom she was in mourning?" said Picard.

Deanna Troi stood still as the voice answered.

"Yeah," said the pilot. "She's in mourning for her daughter."

△ △ △

Picard, Troi, Data, and Riker hurried toward the transporter room. The transporter room doors hissed open. Lwaxana Troi, dressed all in black, was complaining about being kept waiting.

Deanna Troi entered first. The transporter operator, O'Brien, looked very pleased to see her.

She stopped a few feet short of her mother, her hands on her hips.

"Mother," she said in a warning tone.

Lwaxana Troi took no notice of her daughter's anger. She held her hands out and spoke in a sad voice. "My little one—I'm so sorry."

Deanna sighed loudly. She took her mother's hands. "We will talk about this later," she said.

"I imagine we will. Jean-Luc!" Lwaxana turned to the captain. "As handsome as ever."

Picard raised an eyebrow. For a woman in mourning, she certainly could turn it on and off.

"Mrs. Troi," he said. He bowed his head slightly. "Welcome aboard." There was a smile on the captain's face, but he groaned softly. When Deanna's mother showed up, a battle of wits was sure to begin. In a way, Picard liked the game of staying one step ahead of Lwaxana Troi. But at the same time, he could do without the extra work.

In a guest room of the *Enterprise*, Deanna stood before her mother. Her slim body was shaking with anger. "Mother, I will not stand for this!" she said.

Deanna wanted to know why Lwaxana had said she was in mourning for her. Then she sighed. *Explain what this is all about, Mother.*

Lwaxana gave a small smile. "So you can still send. Just wanted to make sure. Deanna, you have to understand. There's nothing I can do. It is the way of our people. It is the Ab'brax."

"Mother! The Ab'brax hasn't been in use for ages. I can't have you saying that you are in mourning for me and acting as if I am dead!"

"Now, now, Little One! You are not dead in the usual sense. It is the hope that you will *ever* find a mate that is dead. The hope that you will bear children and continue our line is dead."

Deanna leaned back. She thumped her head against the wall. "I don't believe this."

"Well, now, there is still that lovely Commander Riker." Lwaxana smiled. "He still wants you, you know. I can read him clear as glass."

"You're still in phase, aren't you, Mother?" Deanna was talking about a time during which older Betazoid women are driven to find a mate.

Lwaxana moved her hand as if to wave away the question. "This isn't about me. It's about you."

"Mother, I'm having a full and happy life."

"Oh, when I think of you all alone, it makes me so sad. I become as blue as when I—" Her voice trailed off.

"As when what, mother? As when you think of yourself?"

"I am perfectly fine, Little One. At least I had my time with your father." Her eyes looked sad for a moment. Then she drew herself up tall. "What do you think I should wear to the party?"

Deanna saw that their talk had ended. "I have work to do," she said. She turned and was almost to the door. Suddenly a voice in her head said, *Little One, aren't you afraid of growing old alone?*

Deanna stopped a moment. Then she thought back, *No, because I'll always have myself.*

Mrs. Troi sighed. *I envy you.*

Deanna went out into the hall. She couldn't help but think how often children grew up and turned into their parents.

# CHAPTER 4

The Ten-Forward lounge was crowded to bursting. Picard walked about smiling at the guests. Suddenly, he felt a bump from behind. It was Graziunas, moving like a bull through the crowd.

"Sorry, Picard!" he boomed cheerfully. "Look at them!" Graziunas laughed and pointed at a table. There were Kerin and Sehra. They were holding hands and looking dreamily at each other.

"Young love, Picard. Remember it?"

A voice broke in before the captain could answer. "Will you share the father of the bride, Jean-Luc?"

Picard turned to see Lwaxana Troi standing uncomfortably close to him. "Pardon me, Mrs. Troi. Graziunas," he said quickly, "do you know—?"

Graziunas took her hands. "Could I forget the daughter of the fifth house? Lwaxana, you are never far from my thoughts. How are you, my dear?"

"Graziunas, you old flirt," replied Lwaxana. "You'll make Jean-Luc jealous."

Graziunas looked from one to the other.

"Captain, are you and the lovely Lwaxana—?"

"Just friends," said Picard quickly.

"Close friends," said Lwaxana Troi.

At that moment the lights in the lounge flickered off, and then on again. There was a strange sound, as if there had been a power drain. Everyone looked around but did not seem alarmed. Space travelers were not upset by a power surge.

Picard, however, did not miss his chance. "I must see to this. Please excuse me. Duty calls."

"Now there is a man who puts his job first," said Graziunas.

Lwaxana frowned. "Yes," she said. She could not hide the sour note in her voice.

Behind the bar, Guinan's eyes went wide. It had been such a little flicker of the lights. Usually she wouldn't pay it any notice. But Guinan knew right away. She looked around quickly, trying to pick *him* out in the crowd. Where was *he*?

Her head snapped around in time to see the doors hiss shut. Someone had indeed entered. But the room was packed. She couldn't see where *he* was.

"Captain!" she called out. She finally saw Picard on the other side of the room. Guinan took a deep breath. She started to push her way through the crowd. All the while, she looked around, trying to pick out the being that she knew was there.

Captain Picard was surprised to see Guinan pushing toward him. She was getting angry looks from people in the crowd. "Some hostess," one person said. Guinan went straight to Picard.

"What's wrong, Guinan?" he asked.

"He's here," she whispered.

Picard frowned for a moment, not able to understand. But then he did. He knew exactly who and what she was talking about. He knew from the way she was acting. She was tense. No one, and nothing, made Guinan tense, except for one being.

"Jean-Luc, what is the matter? You are upset!" Lwaxana Troi had found her way to his side again.

"Nothing to worry yourself about, Lwaxana," said Picard, trying to cover.

"You're concerned over a letter of the alphabet?"

Picard frowned. He had forgotten with whom he was dealing. He turned and faced Lwaxana. "This is not the time for mind reading." Gently, but firmly, he sat her down. "We're all in danger," he told her in a low voice." If you read anything from my mind, read my real concern for you and for this ship. Stay here!"

Picard turned back to Guinan. "Where is he?"

"I don't know," Guinan said.

There was loud laughing from the middle of the room. The two fathers were having a fine time.

Then Picard heard Nistral say, "A cigar in his mouth! Oh, that must have been something!"

"Oh, it was," came another voice. Picard knew it like he knew the sound of nails on a blackboard.

He started through the crowd. He thought of calling security but decided not to. What in the world could they do besides get themselves hurt?

The crowd parted for the captain. Guinan was right behind him. Picard heard three men—well, two men and something else—laughing loudly. He made it through the crowd and stood facing Graziunas, Nistral, and—him.

"Oh, Captain!" said Graziunas. "Your admiral was just telling us some stories about your past. They're probably things you'd rather keep quiet."

"I know just what I'd like to keep quiet," said Picard. He pointed his finger at the figure dressed in a Starfleet uniform. "What I'd like to keep quiet is this person right here!"

"Now, Jean-Luc," said Q, raising his own finger. "Temper, temper!"

🖖 🖖 🖖

Deanna Troi and Worf were on the bridge. Worf had kept his security team away from the party. Picard thought it would help the guests feel more comfortable. But to the Klingon, there was no such thing as being too careful.

Deanna Troi sat at her usual seat on the bridge. She was there for two reasons. First, she knew that her mother was down at the party. She hated this Ab'brax business and wanted to stay away from Lwaxana. The second reason was that crowded parties were hard on her. All the feelings crashed upon her like waves of a flood.

She wished that she had her mother's powers. Lwaxana could easily put up mind screens. They protected her from the feelings of others. She could choose to receive only the feelings she wanted. She was a full Betazoid, with strong powers at that. Deanna was only half-Betazoid.

*Little One,* sounded in Deanna's head.

She blinked in surprise. She sent back, *What is it, mother?*

*I wonder, dear, does the letter Q have any meaning for you?*

Deanna's eyes widened. "*Q!*" she said aloud.

Worf's head snapped up. "*Q?*" he said.

*Mother, why did you bring it up?* Deanna demanded.

*There is the strangest fellow here. Jean-Luc connected him with that letter—*

Deanna got to her feet. "I'll be right down," she said to thin air. "Worf, hurry!"

Worf had no idea what was going on, but he followed her into the lift.

In the lift, Deanna said, "Ten-Forward deck." She turned to Worf. "I believe Q is at the party."

"He picked the wrong one to crash," growled Worf. He touched his communicator. "Worf to security. Meet me at Ten-Forward. Q is there."

🔱 🔱 🔱

"What are you doing here, Q?" demanded Picard.

Q looked hurt. "I? Just enjoying your party, Picard. Is that all right?"

"No, it is not," shot back the captain.

Graziunas looked from Picard to Q. "Captain, is there some problem?" he asked.

"Yes," said Nistral. "Do tell us. The admiral here was being most entertaining—"

"He's not an admiral!" said Picard. "He is—"

But Picard thought, *What now? Can I tell them he is a superbeing who can do anything with just a thought? Shall I let them know this creature can kick us out into space if he wants to? I can't start a panic.*

Picard hoped that Lwaxana Troi wasn't listening in on his thoughts.

"He's not welcome on this ship," Picard said.

Members of the *Enterprise* crew had begun to recognize Q. Many were backing away. Commander Riker pushed his way to Picard's side.

"Captain, I cannot go along with you on this," said Graziunas.

"Yes, Picard. He can't go along," Q told him. He sipped from his glass. Then he looked at it with a frown. Suddenly, the clear liquid turned a deep purple. He smiled and drank.

"This is a Tizarin celebration," Graziunas continued. "We welcome all who come peacefully."

"He is right," said Nistral.

"That may be," said Picard. "But he is not welcome aboard this ship."

"We can't ask him to leave," said Graziunas. That would be bad luck. Why, we would have to stop the wedding."

"Face it, Picard. I'm back," said Q.

"What do you want, Q?" Picard asked.

"Why do you think I want anything?" Q replied.

Suddenly, Q took a step back. Guinan had come close. She crossed her hands in front of herself as if trying to hold him away. Q tensed like a cat. "This is no way to treat a guest, Picard," he said.

"You're no guest here, Q," Picard told him.

Worf chose just that moment to enter. He was backed up by four security guards.

"Worf!" Q greeted him happily.

Worf growled. The sound of an angry Klingon was more than enough to frighten anyone.

The only one who did not seem bothered was Lwaxana Troi. She had watched the whole thing, and she never took her eyes off Q. Deanna was at her side now. She took her mother's arm.

"Mother, come quickly," she said.

Lwaxana did not move. "I'm fine, Little One."

"Mother, you don't understand the danger."

"Hush," said Lwaxana firmly.

Meanwhile, Q was busy with Worf. In a loud voice, he called out, "You'll have to forgive Worf, he's a bit of an animal."

Worf took a step toward him.

"Worf!" said Picard.

"Heel!" Q told him.

Guinan stepped between them. Her eyes were full of fire. Q's lips drew back in an ugly grin. Graziunas and Nistral were talking at the same time. Things were getting out of hand.

"*Enough!*" shouted Picard.

For a moment, there was dead silence.

"Captain, the Tizarin way is quite clear," said Graziunas.

"We can talk about that later," Picard told him. "For now, Q, let's discuss this outside."

"As you wish, Picard," Q replied.

Picard and Q headed for the door. The captain turned and forced a smile. "Enjoy yourselves, everyone. This will only take a moment."

The doors hissed open. "After you, Picard," Q said.

Then Picard and Q stepped outside—the ship.

# CHAPTER 5

Wesley Crusher had never screamed at his post before. He didn't scream this time, really. It was more like he yelped in surprise. He had come on duty early because he didn't feel like going to the party. He hadn't been able to get a date and didn't want to show up alone.

He glanced up at the screen. Picard was on it.

Wesley leaped from his seat, crying out in alarm. The bridge crew looked up. "What's wrong?" came the question. But the questions stopped as soon as the others saw what Wesley was looking at.

Picard was floating dead ahead. He was not just floating, but moving right along with the *Enterprise*. No human could move at such a speed! No human could live in airless space without a space suit. But Picard was doing it!

A thousand questions leaped into Wesley Crusher's mind. One answer came up.

"Q," he said.

He hit his communicator. "Bridge to transporter. O'Brien, this sounds crazy, but the captain is dead ahead."

"The captain?" asked O'Brien.

"Lock on, and beam him back in here," Wesley said.

"Something's wrong!" cried O'Brien, alarmed. "The transporter is not working. It's dead!"

"Bridge to Commander Riker," Wesley said now. "It's the captain. He's in front of the ship."

"What!" answered Riker from Ten-Forward.

"He's dead ahead. Commander, would Q by any chance—?"

"Good guess!" said Riker. "Riker to trans—"

"I already tried that, Commander. The transporter is dead."

"Riker to shuttle bay. Prepare to send out a shuttlecraft. I'm on my way down. Bridge, let me know if anything changes out there. Riker out."

Other members of the bridge crew had gathered around Wesley. They stared at the screen. The captain was waving his arms about as if trying to move. He clearly was not in control of things.

"Tell me about him."

Deanna Troi stared into her mother's eyes. The party had started up again. Luckily, the sliding doors had blocked the sight of the captain and Q disappearing into thin air.

"About whom?" asked Deanna.

"That gentleman who had Jean-Luc so upset."

"Do not think it, mother," said Deanna firmly. "Do not toy with it in your wildest dreams."

Lwaxana Troi patted her daughter's face. "Don't worry, Little One. I can handle myself."

The *Enterprise* was large in front of Picard. He noted how fine his ship was. He also noted he did not feel the icy cold he should have felt floating in space. He was as warm as if he were in his cabin. That he wasn't already dead was a sign that he wasn't going to die, at least not soon.

"Picard," came that voice. "Shall we talk?"

"Q!" the captain shouted. Because he could not speak in airless space, he must have been hearing himself within his own head. "Q, show yourself!"

Q appeared in space next to him, arms folded. "You wished to step outside, Picard."

Picard was trying not to think about the fact that he was at Q's mercy. Whatever the super-being wanted to do to him, he could very easily do. But the *Enterprise* captain had never backed down from him before. He was not going to start now.

"Listen to me, Jean-Luc. You know that the Q took away my powers once before for behaving badly to you human beings. My powers were only recently returned. I am, in your human terms, on parole. My fellow members of the Q are watching me. They think I can be a bit of a bully."

"You are a bully," said Picard. "You do what you want to whomever you want. I'm floating in deep space against my will. What does that tell you?"

"Look." Q pointed. "We're getting company."

A shuttlecraft was moving toward them.

"Jean-Luc, you would give any human a chance to change. Will you give me the same chance? It's a party. Allow me to attend. You heard them. If you insist I leave, they'll consider it bad luck. The wedding will be off. It will be your fault, Jean-Luc, not mine."

Picard blinked. And he was in the shuttle with Worf, Riker, and Data.

"Captain, are you all right?" said Riker.

Picard patted himself up and down. "Quite fit, Number One."

The shuttle sped back toward the *Enterprise*. All the way Riker and Worf worried that Picard would be whisked away once more. They wondered, without much hope, if they had seen the last of Q.

All hope disappeared when they walked into the Ten-Forward lounge a little later. Q was standing there. He was telling about more embarrassing moments that Picard would have rather forgotten.

He turned and waved to the captain. "Jean-Luc! Won't you join us?"

Across the way, Lwaxana Troi was eying Q. If Picard had seen her look, it might have led him to shut down the whole celebration no matter what the Tizarin said. Shut it down and be done with it. But he didn't see; and some horrible meetings are too much for anyone to think about.

Lwaxana Troi came sweeping across the Ten-Forward lounge. As if sensing her coming, Q turned. He raised an eyebrow and watched her.

"Jean-Luc," said Lwaxana. "Who is your charming friend?"

It was then that Picard remembered. Lwaxana was in phase. She was still in search of a mate!

Before he could answer, Q broke in. "I am Q."

"How lovely. Are there any more letters like you at home?" She laughed lightly.

Q smiled.

Picard groaned softly.

"How charming you are. But you look familiar," said Q.

"Possibly you know Deanna Troi," said Lwaxana.

"Of course," said Q. "Your sister, no doubt."

"Oh, honestly," said Mrs. Troi. She turned red and batted Q on the shoulder.

No one ever touched Q! Picard leaped forward. Worf put his hand on his phaser.

There was silence, and then Q laughed.

It was not a pleasant sound, but Lwaxana Troi was charmed by it. "You flatter me," she said. "I'm her mother, Lwaxana."

"Her mother!" said Q.

Picard broke in quickly. "Mrs. Troi, why don't we go for a walk?"

"Not now, Jean-Luc," said Lwaxana. "Can't you see I'm talking?"

*Mother, this has gone far enough. You're asking for trouble.*

*I can take care of myself, Little One. Trouble is no stranger to me.*

Lwaxana shut down communications and said to Q, "The room is getting very warm."

"But you are right, Mrs. Troi," replied Q. "Would you care to step outside?"

"No!" said Picard.

"Jean-Luc, please," Lwaxana said. "Now is not the time for jealousy. You had your chance."

Q smiled at Lwaxana. "Coming, my dear?"

Lwaxana smiled back. "Absolutely."

Deanna, Picard, Riker, and Worf all started to move forward. They wanted to stop Q from walking away with Lwaxana. None of them took a step. Q had frozen them in their places.

*Mother!* Deanna's mind called out.

*Later, Little One,* Lwaxana sent back. With eyes only on Q, she swept out of the Ten-Forward lounge.

The moment they were gone, Picard and the others could move again. Unaware of what had just happened, Graziunas was grinning. "Trust a sharp devil like Q to waltz out of here with the best-looking woman on the ship."

"Alert all security teams," Picard told Worf. "They are to keep an eye out for Q and Mrs. Troi."

"What else, Captain?" asked Deanna.

"That's all for now."

"But my mother—"

"Is a grown woman, Counselor," Picard replied; "and Q is a grown—whatever."

Lwaxana Troi walked next to Q down the hall of the *Enterprise.* Crew members stepped well aside.

"Tell me about yourself," said Lwaxana.

"Very well," said Q. He looked down at his Starfleet uniform. "I am really not a Starfleet admiral," he said. "I am, in fact, a god."

"Oh, really," she said, with a laugh.

"Yes. I am a member of what is known as the Q Continuum. I can do anything."

"Do you know," asked Lwaxana, "the secret of the universe?"

There was a flash. Something appeared in his hand.

She took it from him and studied it. "A nectarine?" she asked.

He nodded. "Wonderful, isn't it? I wouldn't expect someone like you to understand."

"Someone like me?" she asked sharply.

"Someone who is not a god."

She drew herself up. "I am Lwaxana Troi, daughter of the fifth house. I am as close to a god as you will find on this ship."

She tossed the nectarine at him and walked off.

He smiled. Unpleasantly.

"Little One, I understand your worry," said Lwaxana, back in her quarters again.

"No, mother, I don't think you do understand," said Deanna, her arms folded. "You don't know what you are getting into. He's not the man for you!"

"You base that on what? On your perfect love life? Perhaps, Little One, you should take care of yourself before you worry about me."

Lwaxana glanced down at the fruit bowl. Her eyes widened. There was a nectarine sitting there. It had not been there before. "He is fascinating. There is so much about him to find out."

"But he doesn't know how to love someone. He's not human!" Deanna tried to explain.

"Little One," Lwaxana sighed. She ran her fingers through Deanna's hair. "I understand what you are going through. But I can take care of myself, I promise you."

"Mother—" Deanna looked up at her. She made one more final try to get through. "Mother, he thinks of us as insects."

"I doubt that," said Lwaxana. "He just hasn't met the queen bee yet."

# CHAPTER 6

Kerin and Sehra looked at the thick, green rain forest before them. It seemed to go on and on. There were towering cliffs with little caves and winding rivers. The air was thick with mist.

"It's lovely," breathed Sehra.

"It's based on a real planet," said Wesley. "Do you think you might want to hold your wedding in a setting like this? Whatever you want, the holodeck can provide it."

"It's beautiful," said Sehra, "but—"

"But what?" Kerin asked. "It's perfect."

"Mother will say it's too damp," Sehra worried.

"Who's wedding is this, Sehra?" asked Kerin.

"I just want to make everybody happy," she said.

"Just worry about yourself," he told her. "That's who is important here. What would make you happy?"

"What would make me happy is making everyone else happy," Sehra said.

"Sehra!" he shouted, shaking his head.

"Don't shout at me," she snapped. "I don't have to stand here and be shouted at."

They were glaring angrily at each other. Wesley was starting to worry. He'd been given a simple job—let them choose the world they would most like for their wedding. What would the captain think?

"Look guys," said Wesley slowly. "I'm the same age as you two are. I can tell you, if I were taking the big step—marriage and all—I'd be nervous as could be. I'd probably be arguing about all sorts of things—like holodeck backgrounds, for example. The truth of the matter would be that I was scared. But I'd want to know that I had the understanding of the person I was about to marry."

They stared at him. Then Sehra sighed. "You're right, Wesley. I'm sorry, Kerin," she whispered.

"No, I'm the one who should be sorry," Kerin said quickly. Then he looked at Wesley. "You're pretty smart," he said. "Have you ever been married?"

Wesley laughed. "Oh, no."

"Do you have a special girl?"

"No one special," answered Wesley. He wanted to change the subject. "If you guys like this setting, I need to get back up on the bridge."

"Wesley, I really want to thank you for helping us," said Sehra. "We of Graziunas believe very strongly in giving gifts to show our thanks. I'd like to give you something."

"That's really quite all right," said Wesley. "Just glad to help out."

"To turn down a gift would be a great insult," Sehra told him. "You wouldn't want to insult us, would you? Now, I must be getting back home. Mother is having another fitting for my dress."

"Wesley, do you mind if I stay here for a while?" Kerin asked.

Wesley frowned. "I'm not sure if I should. Well, I guess it would be all right. Just remember: If you get into any trouble, all you have to do is ask the computer for help like this." Wesley raised his voice. "Computer, door!" he said.

Just to their right, a waterfall parted. There was the door of the holodeck.

Sehra kissed Kerin good-bye. Then she and Wesley walked through the door. A second later, the door disappeared. Kerin was left alone in the rain forest world.

He walked along, enjoying the warm, misty world. He watched the clouds float above him in the sky. But he missed seeing the very edge of a cliff. Before Kerin knew it, he was falling over the rim.

He fell, but he did not cry out. He was a son of Nistral. A son of Nistral would meet his end—if the end had come—bravely.

The side of the cliff flashed before him as he fell.

Then, suddenly, Kerin stopped. He just hung there in the air. He waved his arms and legs about.

"Well, it appears you've gotten yourself into some trouble."

Kerin twisted around.

A man was standing straight out from the side of the cliff at an impossible angle. His arms were folded, and he was smiling.

"Need some help?" asked Q.

In a second, Kerin was back on firm ground, and Q was introducing himself.

"Thank you for helping me," Kerin said. "Your powers are really something."

"I think you are quite something, young man," said Q.

"Why do you say that?" Kerin asked.

"Well," Q said, "it is really none of my business. But I find it amazing that you choose to spend the little time you have in the galaxy tied down to just one person."

Kerin didn't understand what Q meant at first. Then he smiled. "Oh, Sehra is a very special girl."

"I'm sure she is," said Q, "and I'm sure your marriage is based on a lot more than the physical side of what you call love. It's important that there is more than the physical, all things considered."

"All things? What 'all things' do you mean?" Kerin asked.

"Well," said Q, "She's not going to stay young forever, is she? Bodies are like time bombs. The years tick away, and sooner or later, everything goes. I'll show you, if you don't mind."

Q waved his arm. Sehra appeared in front of them. She was in a flowing white dress.

"Sehra!" Kerin said.

She smiled as Q said, "Oh, it's not her. Not really. It's only an image to make my point. It may happen a little at a time," Q continued. "Usually the hair starts to go first."

Sehra didn't move. Her smile did not fade. But her long, red-streaked hair began to turn gray.

"Then that young, smiling face will start to wrinkle," said Q. "Her loving look will become one of distrust."

The image of Sehra followed Q's words. Kerin's blood ran cold as he saw Sehra looking at him coldly. Her skin was marked with the lines of age.

Q kept going. "Her body will become bent, and her round cheeks will become sharp. These years will come sooner than you think."

Sehra, a stooped, wrinkled old woman, took a step toward him. Her skin was so thin he could almost see her bones. Slowly, she lifted her arm. It was covered with age spots; and loose skin hung from it. She pointed a long, thin finger at him.

Kerin screamed. He stepped back and tripped

over a rock. He fell right into a pool of water. It splashed into his face. When he blinked, the horrible image of Sehra was gone. "Why did you show me that?" yelled Kerin.

"I'm terribly sorry if I upset you," Q said. "That was the furthest thing from my mind. If you wish, I will never show it again, young friend. But that you'll never see it again, that I cannot promise. You see, you're the one who's marrying her."

With a flash of light, Q disappeared.

When Wesley had finished his shift, he headed down to his room. He opened his door, took two steps into the room, and stopped dead.

A young woman was there. She looked to be in her 20s. Her face was blue. She had short red hair and long red eyelashes. A thin, blue gown of some silky material showed every curve of her perfect body.

"I'm a gift from Sehra of Graziunas." She smiled.

In his daydreams, Wesley had always wondered what he would say at a time like this. What was the perfect line?

In a voice quite a bit higher than his normal tone, he said, "Help."

"Deanna is having a hard time right now," Lwaxana Troi was saying to Q. They were alone together in her quarters. "She seems to have quite a problem seeing us together."

"Poor girl," said Q.

"It is difficult for a child when a parent becomes involved with someone else," said Lwaxana.

"Are we involved?" asked Q.

Lwaxana looked up at him and fluttered her eyelashes. "I would say we're definitely something. Unless you have a problem—?"

"Certainly not," said Q. "I find you a most interesting woman, Lwaxana Troi. You are willing to see me for who I am. You are not like the others. They're jealous, you know."

"Who is?"

Q waved his hand. "Picard and the others."

Lwaxana looked into Q's face. "Have you ever been married?" she asked.

"No," said Q. "Marriage is a very human idea. Being together forever takes on new meaning for someone who will really be here forever."

"You'll never die?" she asked.

"Not unless I wish to. Even then, it would be in a way you cannot understand."

"Try to explain it to me."

"I can't. There are no words."

"You forget, I can read minds. Try me."

"Are you serious? Do you really want to deal with the Q idea of death?"

"Dead serious."

"Very well." He raised his hand. Then he reached out and touched Lwaxana's head with one finger.

For a quick moment, Lwaxana felt an inhuman coolness in his touch. Then she felt something more—something that both excited and frightened her.

Then everything went black.

Picard didn't look up from his desk as the signal announced that someone was at the door.

"Come," he said quickly.

Deanna Troi entered. "Captain, I need to talk to you for a moment about—"

Then she gasped. She fell back against a wall. Picard was quickly out of his seat. He helped her to a chair. He was surprised to see she had gone deathly white.

"Mother!" she whispered. And then she passed out

# CHAPTER 7

"Picard to security," the captain snapped. "Security team to Mrs. Troi's room right away."

Deanna was sitting up now. "Mother," she said again.

"It's all right, Counselor," said Picard. "A security team is on its way to make sure your mother is safe."

"I have to go to her!" cried Deanna. She tried to get to her feet, but her legs gave out.

"What happened?" asked Picard.

"I can sense my mother's moods and feelings, as you know," she said. "There was some sort of—I don't have the words to explain it—some sort of overload. It was as if there was too much for her mind to handle."

"Q?" asked Picard.

"It would seem likely," Deanna answered.

Lwaxana felt strong arms around her. "Q?" she whispered.

The world became clear again. She found she was looking at Worf.

She was confused. "Where's Q?"

Lwaxana tried to remember what had happened. But all she could get were some strange thoughts. She had seen something that was more than she could handle. It was wonderful, it was frightening, and her mind had simply shut down to protect itself.

She looked up at Worf and his security team. "I'm fine," she said. "You may leave now."

Worf glared at her. He turned to his men. "We may leave now," he said, with a note of anger in his voice.

"Women!" the Klingon growled when they were out in the hall. He touched his communicator. "Worf to Captain Picard. There is no problem in Mrs. Troi's quarters, and if there was one, she is not telling us about it."

"Worf reports all is well," Picard said to Deanna. He saw that she still looked very worried. "You don't agree with that?" he asked.

"Captain, I am truly frightened for my mother. I'm afraid she has let herself in for more than she can handle. Q does as he pleases, when he pleases. My mother is a very strong and demanding woman. Who knows what she might do to set Q off? I can't make her see that this is crazy. I can't get her to be careful. Maybe you can."

"Me?"

"Yes, she looks up to you."

"She wants me," Picard said, "not that I've ever led her on, as you well know. Why, last time she was here, she made me so uncomfortable that I had to hide away on the holodeck. I am not one to run and hide. I've faced up to some pretty fierce enemies. But your mother drove me into hiding. I'd say that Q has his work cut out for him."

"Please, Captain, just talk to her. Make sure that she is all right."

The captain sighed. "All right, Counselor. Ask your mother if she will have dinner with me this evening. I will talk to her then."

Deanna let out a breath. "Thank you, Captain."

"Don't thank me yet. Your mother can be pretty set in her ways."

Picard pulled at the collar of his dress uniform. He stood in the hall in front of Lwaxana Troi's door.

"Come in," came her voice.

He sighed. "Into the jaws of death—" he muttered. He put a smile on his face and entered.

Lwaxana Troi wore a flowing green gown.

"No black?" asked Picard.

"I still mourn for my daughter," she said. "But for dinner with such a dear friend, Jean-Luc, I had to dress up." Lwaxana held out her hand and Picard kissed it. "Imagine my surprise when Deanna said you wanted to dine with me."

She waved her hand at the table. It was set with fine foods from Betazed. As they sat down, Picard tried not to feel so terribly uncomfortable.

"Jean-Luc," she said.

"Yes, Lwaxana?"

"I believe I have found the man for me."

"Lwaxana," began Picard, "that is very flattering, but—"

But he wasn't able to get the rest of the sentence out. She wasn't paying any attention to him. "Tell me everything," she said, "and I mean everything that you know about—Q."

Picard leaned forward. He could see he was going to have to talk some sense into her. "As far as we can tell, there is nothing that is beyond Q's powers. That, Lwaxana, should be more than enough to make you see that this cannot possibly work."

"I don't see any such thing," said Lwaxana. "I find powerful men exciting."

"I'm sure they can be exciting. But so is disarming a bomb. One wrong move, and you've had it."

"Oh, you sound just like Deanna, Jean-Luc. I thought better of you."

"I sound like Deanna because we are both right. Q has something up his sleeve. He thinks he can use the crew of this ship for amusing experiments. He has acted very badly in the past. The Q Continuum even took away his powers for a time."

"Jean-Luc," said Lwaxana Troi, "I do believe that you are jealous. You know, Q said that you might be." She patted his hand. "I should have listened to him."

"I am not jealous!" said Picard. "He is dangerous. I want you to be safe. I understand that he caused you to faint dead away earlier today."

"That was not his fault, really. He shared things with me that I wasn't ready for. I asked for too much too soon. I know what's wrong with you, Jean-Luc. You can't stand the thought of me with another man."

Picard stood. "I can see this is not getting anywhere," he sighed. "Good night, Mrs. Troi."

"Now, Jean-Luc. We can still be friends."

Not trusting himself to say another word, Picard turned and walked out of the room.

Lwaxana sighed. "Poor dear," she said.

Deanna was on the bridge when the captain entered. She saw the look on his face.

"It did not go well, I take it," she said.

"Her mind is made up," said Picard. "Your mother is a lonely woman. She wants to believe that she has found the right mate. She will do anything rather than admit that he is not right for her."

"Captain, what are the chances that Q has changed? Could he have feelings toward my mother? Could he really be trying to live by the human ideas of love and understanding? Is there any chance of that at all?"

"I suppose anything is possible," he said. "I honestly don't know. You don't want me to lie to you, do you?"

Deanna wanted to shout, *Yes! Lie to me! Tell me my mother will be all right.*

"Of course not," Deanna said.

In the family ship of the Graziunas, Sehra looked at herself in a tall mirror. Her blue and orange dress swirled about her. Her hair was shining.

She wanted to look her best that evening for Kerin. She had spoken to him earlier on the ship-to-ship communicator. He had sounded uneasy and somehow different. His words were brief and forced. It was the strangest thing.

She turned around suddenly. Something had caught her eye. She looked at her mirror again. All she saw was herself. Yet, just for a moment—she was sure that she had seen a man in a Starfleet uniform. He even looked like someone she had seen before. But that was crazy. What would a Starfleet officer be doing in her mirror?

When Kerin appeared in the transporter room of the *Enterprise*, Sehra was there waiting. The sight of her took his breath away. She stood with her hands folded in front of her. She looked very beautiful. Kerin's parents stood on either side of him, as Sehra's did with her. They all were smiling.

Then, just for a moment, a picture of what Q had shown him flashed in his mind.

Just like that, the mood was broken, and Kerin felt uneasy. The others in the room could sense the change. It passed over him like a dark cloud.

Kerin bowed slightly. He held out a hand politely. Sehra took it. She looked at his face, trying to understand what was wrong.

The two young people walked out of the transporter room in silence. The four parents watched them go.

# CHAPTER 8

Lwaxana checked her fancy headpiece. It was a large thing with winglike sides of black metal. It had been handed down from mother to daughter for hundreds of years. To tell the truth, she felt like she was wearing a spaceship on her head. But once again, it was a matter of tradition.

Her black dress hugged her body, and she ran her hands along her hips. Not bad. Not bad at all. She was sure to be a hit at the celebration party.

She went to her jewelry box and opened it. What to wear, what to wear?

"I have just the thing," she said to herself.

She turned quickly. Q was standing right behind her in the dress uniform of a Starfleet officer.

"I'm sorry for what happened," Q said. He was talking about the dead faint he'd left Lwaxana in earlier that day. "I hope this will help."

Q held out a necklace that was beautiful beyond belief. Lwaxana's eyes widened. The jewels shone like tiny suns.

"Will you accept this small gift?" he asked.

"I'm honored," Lwaxana breathed. "Would you mind putting it on me?"

"I would be most happy to," said Q. He did not touch her, but a second later, the necklace was around her neck.

"It's the most splendid thing I've ever seen," she said. Then she added, "Aside from you."

The dance was already in full swing when Picard arrived with Dr. Crusher on his arm.

A special setting had been created for the party. The walls, the ceiling, even the floor looked like a huge field of stars. People were, it appeared, dancing in space.

The captain and Beverly Crusher stepped onto the dance floor.

Picard saw Kerin dancing with some girl from the house of Nistral. The young man seemed to have eyes only for her. Standing off to the side, looking very unhappy, was Sehra.

"That," said Picard, "is not good."

"Oh, they're young," said Crusher. "They'll work it out."

"I hope so. We have heavily armed ships on either side of us. They are manned by families with a longtime feud. We don't need any problems!"

Deanna and Riker entered. Deanna looked quickly around and said, "I don't see them here."

Riker sighed. "Are you going to spend the evening worrying about your mother? Let's dance."

Just then Wesley Crusher came in. On his arm was the blue-skinned woman with the red hair. The captain had agreed to give the girl a room on board the *Enterprise*. She could stay there until Wesley figured out how to return Sehra's "gift" politely. Wesley nodded in the direction of the other young men. They stood with their mouths open. "Gentlemen," he said simply. Then he took the girl in his arms and twirled her onto the dance floor.

She stepped on his foot.

"Sorry," she whispered.

"No problem," he gasped back, trying to stop a cry of pain.

Suddenly, there was a blinding flash of light. People held their hands up to protect their eyes. From within the heart of the light, two figures began to take shape. It was Q and Lwaxana Troi.

Lwaxana was holding Q's arm tightly. "Does he know how to make an entrance, or what?" she said.

Deanna put her hand to her head and moaned.

Q held out his arms. "Lwaxana, would you care to dance?"

Deanna walked quickly to Picard. "Captain," she said, "stop them."

"What can I do, Counselor?"

"I don't know," she said, "and I hate not knowing."

Kerin was watching Q when he heard a voice at his side. He turned, and there was Sehra.

"You haven't danced with me," she said, "not the whole evening."

"I've been busy," he said.

"Busy with every other girl here," she replied. Tears came to her eyes.

Kerin began to feel like a creep.

"Oh, Sehra, I'm sorry," he sighed. "I'm just trying to be polite to everyone. The other girls don't mean a thing."

"Are you sure they don't mean anything to you?"

"You are the only girl I think of." He ran his fingers through her long hair. "That's the truth."

She smiled at that, happy again. Then she turned and laughed. "Oh, Kerin, look!"

She dragged him across the dance floor. "Wesley!" she called out.

"I hope you like Karla, my gift to you," she said when they had reached Wesley's side. Karla was hanging on to Wesley tightly. It seemed she was always hanging on to him.

"She's been a good servant," Sehra told Wesley. "It broke my heart to give her away. But the mark of a good gift is that it pains you to give it."

"There is just a little problem, though," said Wesley. "You see—"

"I hope you are not refusing her." Sehra frowned. "That would be a big insult to me."

"It could lead to war with the Tizarin," Kerin added, smiling.

Karla hugged Wesley tight. He looked at Kerin and Sehra. "Let me get back to you," he sighed.

Q turned across the dance floor. Lwaxana felt so comfortable in his arms, so light on her feet. Then she heard the crowd gasp.

When Lwaxana looked about, she gasped, too. They were dancing in midair, high among the "stars." The rest of the guests were looking up and pointing in surprise.

Inside Lwaxana's head, she heard, *Mother!*

*I'm fine, Little One,* she sent back. *Never better.*

"Do you trust me, Lwaxana Troi?" Q asked suddenly. "Do you?"

"Yes," she said firmly.

"Good." With that, he danced her right through the wall of the holodeck. There was a popping sound, and they were gone.

"I'll kill him," said Deanna Troi.

"Breathtaking, isn't it, Lwaxana," said Q.

She looked around at the stars that whirled about her. These were real stars. "It's like a dream," Lwaxana whispered.

She should have been cold. She should have been dead. Instead, there was only the silence of space. Here she was, outside the ship. She was in the arms of one who was greater still than space. And he was sharing his power—and himself—with her.

They twirled faster and faster amid the stars. Lwaxana's eyes were wide. She heard a low laugh— the sound of Q. For a moment, just a moment, the laugh sounded wicked. Then it passed, and she was swept away. The stars were everywhere—in her eyes, in her body, and in her mind. She closed her eyes, gasping, reaching out. Then she heard something—a low rumble, a soft humming.

Slowly, almost fearfully, her eyes opened. She was in her own room. Q was nowhere in sight. She let out a long breath. Then she looked down at the necklace that still hung from her neck. It was shining like the stars. She shook her head. "He certainly knows how to show a woman a good time," she said.

Sehra sat in her room, staring at the walls. Kerin had said he was sorry. But there had still been something wrong. She could not put her finger on it. She threw herself down on her bed. Then she sat up again, staring at the tall mirror across from her. She looked at herself.

She hated what she saw. Her nose was too long. Her forehead was too high. Her hair hung there like string. She was fat. Fat and ugly.

She threw her pillow at the mirror.

An arm came out of the mirror and caught it.

She gasped. She made little noises but couldn't get out a word.

Her own image was gone from the mirror. In its place was the image of—of that man! It was the one from the party, the one who had been dancing through the air.

"You should be more careful," he said. He put first one leg, then the other, into her room. Then he stepped completely out from the glass.

"How," she gasped. "How did you—" Her voice faded for a moment. "Are you a magician?"

"In a sense," said Q. "My magic is understanding what makes people tick. My dear child," he said, "I am both a great teacher and a great student. I try to learn and understand."

"What can I teach you?" she asked.

"I am most interested in the idea of loving one, and only one, person."

"Yes," she said slowly. "We Tizarin believe in staying with one person for life."

"I don't understand," Q said. "If you meet another person who is attractive to you, you cannot love that person?"

"Not in the same way. We believe in 'one man, one woman,'" she said.

"So your Kerin loves you, and you alone?"

"Oh, yes."

"Odd. That is not what I saw."

She frowned. "What do you mean?"

"Well, your boyfriend Kerin seemed to have some other things on his mind this evening."

Q pointed to the mirror. Sehra turned to look at it. She gasped.

There was Kerin. His arms were around a girl from Nistral.

"I don't believe it," she said firmly.

The Nistral girl faded. Another appeared.

"You're making this up," Sehra said. But this time, her voice was less sure.

"This one, then?" he asked, and there was Kerin dancing with yet another girl. "This was all in his mind tonight. I didn't make it up. I just wanted to know if this was what you meant by his being only interested in you. Or maybe this is." Another girl appeared, "or this, or this, or—"

"Stop it!" Sehra screamed. "Stop it! Stop saying these things! Kerin loves me. He does!"

"Oh, I'm certain," said Q. "Although it is strange. He pictures all these girls except you. It's as if you hold no mystery."

"I think you are doing nothing but lying!"

"Nobody, dear girl," said Q, "can lie quite as well as we do to ourselves." He tipped an imaginary hat at her. "Good day," he said, and he stepped back into the mirror. In an instant, he was gone. The only thing left in the mirror was the tear-covered face of a teenage bride-to-be.

# CHAPTER 9

Wesley heard a light knock on his door. When it slid open, there was Karla. "Good morning, Wesley," she said brightly. "I brought you breakfast." Karla brushed his neck and shoulder with her hand as she put down the breakfast tray. "You are so tense," she said. "Let me help. I give great back rubs." She began to rub his shoulders and his neck.

"Hey, that feels really good," Wesley said.

"You'll have to lie down on the floor and watch what I can really do," Karla said. Before Wesley could question her, Karla had taken off her shoes and was walking carefully across his back.

Wesley let himself relax. Actually, this did feel good. It felt really—

A few minutes later, Wesley Crusher was howling with pain, and Karla was helping him toward his mother's sickbay.

"You must hate me," she cried. "I'm so sorry." Poor Karla had broken a couple of Wesley's ribs.

Ten-Forward was empty, except for Guinan. As near as anyone could tell, she never left.

There was a bright flash, and Q appeared. "What does one have to do to get a drink around here?" he said.

Guinan shook her head. "I'm not going to serve you, Q."

"You call yourself a hostess."

"These are good people," said Guinan from behind the bar. "Why do you want to hurt them?"

"How am I hurting anyone? I have been on my best behavior."

The door of Ten-Forward hissed open. Deanna Troi entered. "I knew you'd come here," she said. "It's over, Q."

He raised an eyebrow. "Whatever do you mean?"

"I can read you." She took a step forward. "I can sense every rotten thought that goes through your mind."

"No, you can't," he said calmly. "My mind is a closed book to you."

"It's an open book. It seems your powers are less than you think."

Q did not like what he was hearing. There was danger in his eyes.

"I know your every move," Deanna went on. "You plan to embarrass my mother, to use her. You are setting her up for a fall just to show that you can do it. Your every move is plain to me."

"You're lying!" Q's voice was hard and angry.

"I don't have to lie. I'm here to tell you that I'm not afraid of you. I love my mother. If you hurt her, I will make sure that you pay."

"You!" He started to shake with anger. "You think you can threaten me! You—you—"

"I will step on you," she said quietly, "like the bug that you are."

He took a step toward her. His eyes were on fire.

Guinan jumped between them. Just what Guinan could possibly do against Q, Deanna couldn't guess. But the Ten-Forward hostess seemed to have something in mind.

What that might have been, Deanna Troi would never know. As suddenly as the storm had gathered, it passed. Q's anger was gone. Within seconds he was calm again.

"You say you love your mother. Well, she is happy with me. Would you take that happiness away?"

With those words, Q disappeared.

Deanna sighed and sank down in a chair.

Guinan walked over to her. "You couldn't read him?"

"No," said Deanna.

"It was a bluff?"

"Yes."

"Mind telling me why?"

"Because," said Deanna, "if he had attacked me, hurt me—my mother would have been aware of it. I wanted her to see just what Q can do."

"In other words, you were willing to risk yourself for your mother."

Deanna shrugged. "Guinan, is it possible that he is telling the truth? Could he have changed?"

"I was wondering that earlier. Frankly, I don't think so. The only question is, how much hurt is he going to cause while he's spinning his lies?"

🚀 🚀 🚀

The quarrels were becoming louder. They came more often. There were cold looks and out-and-out anger. Everyone among the Tizarin was beginning to wonder if this was more than simple prewedding jitters.

No one could figure out what was wrong. But something had happened. Kerin looked at Sehra with a cool eye. Sehra looked at Kerin with doubt.

At night, a voice whispered warnings into Kerin's ear, and it whispered uncertainty into Sehra's ear. It spoke words of affection to Lwaxana Troi.

That night, Graziunas and Nistral were visited as well. The visits came as a dream. In the morning, they awoke with their hearts hardened toward each other and their tempers ready to flare.

The traditional prewedding ceremonies were due to begin shortly. The holodeck had created the rain forest setting that the couple had chosen. But the forest was empty now, except for two figures. Q and Lwaxana Troi stood at the edge of a cliff looking over the jungle.

Q was eating a nectarine. He sighed loudly. "Your daughter—everyone on board this ship, really—would love to take your freedom away from you. They don't want you to be with me. They want to keep you from love."

"Are you saying you love me?" Lwaxana's voice was a whisper.

"Need you ask?"

Lwaxana sighed.

"You can have all that I have shown you," said Q. "I offer you everything. I warn you though; if you accept my offer, you will see the others for what they really are. They will seem small and unimportant to you."

"Will you tell me why a nectarine holds the answer to the secrets of the universe?"

"My dear," he said, "you won't even have to ask. So—do you want it?" He took her hands. "Are you ready to leave behind the small worries of the others and join me?"

"I—I don't know," she said. "I mean, it's such a big step. I—"

The waterfall nearby hissed open.

Lwaxana pulled her hands from Q as she spun around. Standing there were Picard, Riker, Deanna, and all the members of the Tizarin wedding party. Deanna showed surprise as Picard said, "Mrs. Troi! Ready for the prewedding ceremonies to begin?"

Lwaxana's face turned red. She felt as if she'd been caught in the act of something. "Oh, yes," she said. "We certainly are."

"We?" said Picard, looking around. Lwaxana looked behind her. Q was gone. She turned back to the captain and tried to smile.

"Yes, of course," said Picard. He didn't quite understand Lwaxana's jumpiness. But at least Q wasn't around. The ceremony could go smoothly, and tomorrow would be the wedding. They could be done with this business.

It took only ten minutes after the beginning of the ceremony for the storm to break loose.

# CHAPTER 10

Picard smiled at those gathered before him. The Tizarin all wore colors that declared their house. The other guests stood off to the side.

The captain flipped through the Tizarin book of ceremonies. He wanted to get an idea of how long the prewedding ceremony would last. He sighed. It was at least 30 pages long.

"Good people!" he read. "All who have come together this day in this place—" He looked around the holodeck rain forest.

"If they can stand the damp," whispered Fenn.

"Mother!" breathed Sehra. "I *told* you—"

"Sorry," Fenn whispered back.

"I knew she'd cause problems," said Kerin.

"Kerin, she's my mother," Sehra shot back.

Picard frowned and went on. "This love will last forever, through old age and beyond—"

Kerin made a small noise. It was like a choke.

Sehra turned to him and said, "What do you mean by that?"

"By what?"

"By that noise you just made."

Graziunas stepped forward. "Sehra, there are people here."

"I want to know what that noise he made was."

"I didn't make a noise!" said Kerin. "I was just coughing."

Now Nistral came toward them. "He just coughed, Sehra. That's all."

"Of course, you'd take his side," said Sehra.

"Gentlemen, ladies," began Picard, "if there is a problem here—"

"There is no problem," Kerin said. He fired a look at Sehra. "Is there, Sehra?"

"I will thank you," Fenn said, "not to take that tone with my daughter!"

"What tone?" Nistral said. "The boy didn't do anything. Why does that daughter of yours nag him?"

Picard closed the book with a bang. "That's it. This goes no further. You can't seem to—"

Kerin broke in. "Look, Sehra. If you have a problem with me, I don't see why you have to drag your parents into it!"

"I don't drag my parents anywhere. They go where they please and do what they please."

"Then maybe I should do the same thing!" shouted Kerin.

The wedding parties of each house began to move toward their house leaders.

"You'll never be able to see other women! That's what's eating at you, isn't it!" snapped Sehra.

"No!" answered Kerin. "It's that I'm going to have to see you at all!"

Sehra stepped back as if he had hit her. Now Graziunas moved forward. "How dare you!"

"She pushed him to it, that's how he dares," cried Nistral.

"That's enough!" snapped Riker. It was like trying to stop a flood after the dam had broken.

Picard tapped his communicator. "Security team to Holodeck 3, now!"

"Liars!" yelled Graziunas.

"Bullies!" cried Nistral.

The air was filled with shouting. Just as Worf and the security team charged in, Graziunas swung an angry punch. It hit Nistral square in the mouth. The leader of the house of Nistral went down. Kerin jumped forward and leaped on the back of Graziunas. Sehra screamed as her father went down, too.

People were slamming into each other. They were pushing and yelling. It took the security team several minutes to quiet things down. Then, in a voice as clear and calm as possible, Picard said, "Get off my ship. All of you. You will not be welcome again until you cool down."

Nistral took a step forward. Blood covered his

face. He poked a finger at Graziunas. "We have no need of your ship, Captain. We need only our own, and what we need it for, we will quickly finish."

"Blood feud," growled Graziunas. "You have had it coming for a long time, Nistral."

"Blood feud it is," shot back Nistral. "I have put up with you for the sake of our young ones. But I will stand for you no longer!"

"Let us out of here, Captain!" shouted Graziunas. "We have things to take care of."

"I want you to cool off." Picard began.

"It's no longer your business, Captain," said Nistral. "It's ours to settle, and we will. I suggest you get your ship to a safe distance. Very shortly, there is going to be a fight."

Within minutes, the Tizarin had emptied out of the holodeck. The *Enterprise* officers and a group of surprised guests stood looking at each other.

Lwaxana Troi came forward. Her lip was bleeding. It had been cut in all the fighting.

"Anyone for coffee and cake?" she asked.

"The question is, what should we be doing?"

Picard faced his officers in the meeting room. His question hung in the air. No one had a ready answer.

"The Federation's Prime Directive is clear," said

Riker. "We can ask the Tizarin to settle this peacefully. We can help them set up meetings. But we can't twist their arms. It is not our place to force anything."

Worf spoke up. "It might be best to move our ship. We are sitting right between the Tizarin house ships. We could be caught in the cross-fire."

"But by staying here," said Picard, "we send a clear message. We say we want to see this settled right away. You know," the captain continued, "I don't understand. Why did they all have such short tempers?" His eyes narrowed. "What are the chances that Q had something to do with this?"

"Captain, Q wasn't there," Riker pointed out.

"I don't know," said Picard. "Perhaps he was there in spirit. All I know is that the Tizarin are in a state of war, and I'm looking for reasons."

"Perhaps, Captain," said Data slowly, "Q was not there because whatever he had done, he had already taken care of."

"I don't follow, Mr. Data," said Picard.

"It is entirely possible that—"

Suddenly, an alarm sounded. Everyone rose.

"Hold that thought, Mr. Data," said Picard. "It seems matters are moving ahead without us."

The officers stepped onto the bridge. "Shields are up, sir," reported a crew member. "The Tizarin ships have begun to fire at each other."

The *Enterprise* rocked.

"A hit," Data reported. "It appears to be a stray shot rather than one aimed at us."

"Get us out of here," said Picard. "Circle the two ships. We want them to know we're still here."

"What difference will that make?" asked Riker.

"Frankly, Number One," said Picard unhappily, "probably not one bit."

Sehra lay on her bed, sobbing. Beside her sat Karla, who had also returned to the Graziunas ship. She was patting Sehra's back.

"How did it all go wrong?" Sehra cried. "What happened? First, one thing was said, and then another."

"I don't know, mistress," Karla said. "I don't know much of anything, I'm afraid. I didn't even know how to make Wesley Crusher happy."

"This is all my fault," Sehra sobbed. "I want things back the way they were! I can't live knowing that all this is happening because of me! I don't want to go on. I just want Kerin!" Sehra sat up. "Leave me alone now, Karla. I need to be alone."

Karla squeezed Sehra's hand. Shaking her head sadly, she left the room.

When the door shut, Sehra looked into her mirror. She saw a frightened, angry young woman.

"If I can't have Kerin," she said, "then I don't want myself, either. There is no point in living without him. I've been such a fool. Even if I went to him now, he would probably hate me. No, it's better this way."

She pushed a button and Karla was at the door in a second. "Do you want me again, mistress?"

"Yes, Karla," said Sehra. Her voice sounded stronger now. "I want you to go down to the ship's storeroom. Get a fighter uniform and a helmet. Bring them quickly. Tell no one on the ship about any of this."

"But—"

"Do as I say."

"Yes, mistress," said Karla. "Whatever you say."

Kerin stood on the flight deck of the Nistral ship. He was dressed in full fighting gear. His father came toward him. "Ready, son?"

"Father, when I flew to the Graziunas ship to win Sehra's hand, I felt so sure of myself. I never could have made it if I had felt the way I do now."

"I understand, son. You loved this girl, or thought you did. Now you will fight her family."

"I didn't think I loved her, father. I know I just do—did—do—" He shook his head.

"It's not your fault, Kerin. You had second thoughts, and she became a nagging witch."

"She didn't!" Kerin cried. "She's beautiful and young. Who cares what she'll look like years from now?"

His father looked at him hard. He spoke with a voice of iron. "Kerin, we have gone along with your wishes in every way. When you wanted to marry her, I backed you. When the arguments began, I backed you. Graziunas has been a bully for too long. I've always wanted to pound some sense into him. If I have to blow him to dust to do it, then that's what I'll do. But you can't start having second thoughts again. We've gone too far. Our forces are ready."

"Can't we call them off?" said Kerin.

"No! Kerin, someday you will carry the name of Nistral. You will be the leader. Do you think that anyone will follow a man who can't make up his mind? Now, get ready to fly."

Kerin, the future Nistral—should he live that long—hung his head. "Yes father," he said.

Sehra climbed into the fighter ship. She pushed a button. The hatch slid closed over her head with a click. It felt like a coffin.

She had not flown in ages and then only under

her father's eye. But thanks to the big helmet and loose jumpsuit, no one had noticed her on the flight deck.

Sehra fired up the main engines. Her ship pulled forward. It was not so hard. Much of the work was done by the computer, and she remembered everything she had learned.

"This," she said, "is to make up for starting the mess. This is to make up for losing the best thing I ever had." The ship, with a final roar of the engines, flew into the silence of space.

"Captain, we're getting a message from the Graziunas ship," said Worf.

"This is Captain Picard. Graziunas, I—"

A girl's voice came over the air. "Uhmm—is Wesley Crusher there?"

"Who is this?" demanded Picard.

"My, uhmm, my name is Karla. I have to speak to Wesley right away."

"Young lady, this is the bridge of the *Enterprise*," said Picard sternly. "We do not allow personal calls. Worf, cut off the—"

"It's an emergency!" came the frightened voice. "I have to talk to Wesley. It's a matter of life and death!"

"Captain, perhaps—" said Deanna Troi.

"Yes, yes, anything. Just get her off the air," said Picard.

Deanna took over the call. "Computer, transfer incoming message to Wesley Crusher."

At that moment, Wesley Crusher lay in sick bay, resting his broken ribs. On the next bed sat Lwaxana Troi. She was having her cut lip patched up after the prewedding ceremony.

Wesley's communicator beeped and he touched it. "Crusher here."

"Wesley? Wesley, is that you?"

His eyes widened. "Karla? *Karla!* How did you get to me?"

"The man on the bridge connected us—"

"You called the *bridge* looking for me?"

"Wesley, it's Sehra! She's going to be killed! She made me promise not to tell any of her people. I can't go against her wishes. But I can tell you. You have to do something! She has gone out on a fighter ship. She won't last five minutes!"

"I'll do what I can!" said Wesley.

"Thanks Wesley. I knew you'd help! Good-bye!" said Karla.

"Wait! Wait! Darn—Crusher to bridge."

"Are you done visiting with your girlfriend, Mr. Crusher?" The captain did not sound happy.

"Sir, Sehra is in a fighter ship. Her parents don't know about it. She will be killed!"

"A lot of the Tizarin are going to be killed, Mr. Crusher. But we'll let them know. Maybe it will make a difference. Bridge out."

But when Captain Picard tried to hail the Tizarin ships, they would not receive his message.

Kerin dove through the air. He dodged blasts of fire. His shields were holding, but a few more attacks would take care of that.

Then he noticed something. One of the Graziunas ships had broken off from the others. It was headed toward the house ship of Nistral at top speed. Kerin's computer told him that the ship didn't have any shields.

He tried to come up with a reason for it. He couldn't find one. It must be some sort of trick.

He set off after the Graziunas ship.

Sehra was lost. She couldn't see the other ships. She couldn't see—

There! Ahead of her was a house ship. It took a second for her to see that it was, in fact, the Nistral ship. She tried to reset her course, but she was losing control. It was getting hard to breathe. The ship seemed to be closing in on her.

A warning light flashed. She wasn't sure what it

meant. Then she looked up. A Nistral fighter ship was bearing down on her.

*I'm going to die,* she thought. *I'm really going to die. Oh, gods. Kerin, I'm sorry.*

Suddenly, she didn't want to die. Her shields would protect her long enough to get out of there—Shields! She hadn't put up the shields.

"Make them stop fighting, Q!" Lwaxana begged. "You have the power! You can do it!"

"Of course I could," Q told her. "The problem is, I mustn't. I've sworn to my fellow Q that I would not use my powers in the matters of humans."

"That girl is going to die!" said Lwaxana, "and hundreds more. Please! You must stop them."

"I can't," said Q.

Lwaxana put her head in her hands.

Then Q said slowly, "However—"

She looked up hopefully. "However, what?"

"You are under no such rules, are you?"

Kerin spun toward the Graziunas ship. He was about to kill one of Sehra's family.

He had no choice. The Graziunas fighter was headed right toward the Nistral ship. It had to be stopped.

Kerin got the ship in his sights. "I'm sorry," he whispered.

Sehra reached toward the button to put up her shields. Before she could press the button, there was a flash just above her. She knew what was about to happen.

"I'm sorry," she whispered.

Kerin's blasters spit out death. Kerin's aim was perfect. The diving ship below him was blown to pieces. Bits of it flew out into space. Of the pilot of the ship, there was nothing left.

# CHAPTER 11

On the bridge of the *Enterprise* there was a flash of light. Picard was on his feet. "Q!"

It wasn't Q.

"Mother?" exclaimed a surprised Deanna Troi.

Lwaxana Troi stood before them. She was smiling. There was a soft glow about her.

"Hello, my dear," said Lwaxana. She looked somehow different. Her voice seemed to come from everywhere at once.

Riker spoke first, saying what everyone had just realized. "He's given her the power of the Q."

"Oh, Mother," cried Deanna. "You have no idea what can happen to you."

"Of course I do, dear. I will be all-powerful and do great good."

"Or great evil," said Worf darkly.

"Nonsense." Lwaxana waved her hand. "Just because I have powers doesn't mean I'm no longer a nice person. In fact, I've already taken action."

"Taken action?" said Deanna. "Mother, what are you talking about?"

"Captain," Data said suddenly. "The fighting has stopped. In fact, the Tizarin fighter ships are no longer in space. They have disappeared."

Picard turned toward Lwaxana. "Mrs. Troi," he said very slowly. "Where are the ships?"

"I put them back where they started. It was easy. I just thought it and—poof—it was done."

"Mother, you can't do that! You can't just step into the middle of people's business and—"

"No, Little One, *you* can't step in. I can do whatever I wish."

Kerin was taking off his helmet when his father ran up to him. "What are you doing here?" he shouted. "How did all the ships get back?"

"I don't know," said Kerin. "I have no idea."

Sehra opened her eyes. She expected to find herself in the afterlife. But she had not thought that it would look exactly like her own room.

The door opened, and Karla entered. "I knew that Wesley Crusher could do it!" she cried out.

"Captain Picard," Worf said, "incoming message from the Nistral. There's one from the Graziunas as well. They are angry. They think we used our transporters to send back their fighters."

"They should be thankful!" exclaimed Lwaxana. "I stopped them from killing each other! I stopped that boy from blowing his girlfriend to bits."

"Worf, tell Graziunas and Nistral to gather their families. I want them to meet here on the *Enterprise*," snapped Picard.

Graziunas and Nistral glared at each other across the meeting table. Lwaxana Troi had just shown them her powers. With a blink of the eye, she had made Nistral disappear and then reappear.

"She has interfered. She has broken Federation rules," snapped Nistral. "Her actions were unspeakable."

"Her actions saved lives!" Picard snapped back. He turned to Graziunas. "She saved the life of your daughter!"

"My daughter?" said Graziunas. "What are you talking about?"

Lwaxana pointed at Kerin. "She was in a ship, and he blew it to pieces."

Kerin and Sehra stared at each other. Together they said, "That was *you*?"

"Sehra, if I had—" Kerin couldn't even get the words out. "If I had—"

"I didn't want to live!" she cried.

"I don't care what happens!" said Kerin. "I don't care what you look like when you're old!"

"I don't care if you think about other girls! I just want you!" said Sehra.

"Not again!" shouted Nistral. "First, it's on; then it's off. I won't stand for this!"

"It's what I'd expect from your son!" yelled Graziunas. "He hasn't a mind of his own!"

"Shut up!" shouted Kerin. He grabbed Sehra's hand. "We've listened to all of you. We've listened to everything except our own hearts. No more!"

Nistral and Graziunas started to get up. Both were angry and red in the face.

"That's all!" said Picard. His voice rang. "It seems that these young people have more brains than their parents. I don't want to hear about your feuds or about your houses. We started out with a loving young couple, and we ended up with anger and hatred. Now, what do you call that sorry mess?"

"Why, Jean-Luc!" came a voice like the screech of bats. "It's what you humans call *love*."

Q had appeared in the middle of the meeting table. He stood above them, arms folded.

"That's the man who showed me that you were

going to be old and ugly," said Kerin. "I didn't know how to deal with it."

"He told me that all you cared about was other women!" cried Sehra.

"Q!" said Picard angrily. "So you have been mixing in after all!"

"Is pointing out the truth mixing in?" demanded Q. "I did these young people a favor."

"Kerin and Sehra," said Picard. "In years to come, you both will age. You will grow old together. When you look at each other, you will see the person you've shared many happy years with."

"Pretty words, Picard!" said Q. "Try to explain it as best you can. But it all boils down to one truth. The human idea of love is a joke."

Lwaxana's dark eyes were troubled. "Q, I don't understand what you're saying."

"Woman, you could never understand me," Q said coldly.

Lwaxana gasped. She stepped back.

"This whole ship was filled with the spirits of love, love, love. It was sickening. You humans are always looking for it. I decided to make you see just how silly it is."

Lwaxana was white. " But you said that—"

"Are you deaf and stupid, woman?" asked Q. "How clear can I make it? You have been just one bit of information for my study. I wanted to see how, in the name of love, you would treat your own daughter. I wanted to see how you would fool yourself. *Dear* Lwaxana, you are nothing to me."

"Q, get out of here," ordered Picard.

"A joke," Lwaxana whispered. "It's all been a joke." Suddenly, her voice became stronger. "He gave me the powers of the Q," she said evenly. There was something dangerous in her face.

"Mother," Deanna said, "let's go."

"A joke!" Now when Lwaxana spoke, it was like thunder. "A plot to embarrass me. You no good—" Her face darkened. "You used me! You made me look like a fool!" Slowly, she started toward him.

Q looked a bit surprised. "Lwaxana, give me the powers back. You cannot keep them."

The air crackled around Lwaxana.

"Mother?" said Deanna nervously.

Q seemed suddenly nervous, too. "Lwaxana," he said, "I don't know what you're doing. But you can't have the powers anymore. Now, you're making me angry. Give them back. This is my last word—"

Lwaxana Troi blew him right through the wall of the *Enterprise*.

In a blink, she was outside the ship, behind him. "Q!" she shouted. Energy leaped from her arms. It circled Q, and he screamed. His body snapped about like a puppet. Then he disappeared.

"You can't get away!" shouted Lwaxana Troi, and she disappeared as well.

There was a lot of noise in a hall of the *Enterprise*. Picard, Riker, Worf, and Data came running. Q had appeared, but he was only six inches tall. He was running about on the floor.

Lwaxana stood over him. "Hello, darling," she snarled. Then they disappeared again.

"Computer," said Picard, "find Lwaxana Troi."

"Lwaxana Troi is in the rocketball court."

Lwaxana swung the paddle surely. She smashed Q against the wall. He bounced back to her. With a strong backhand, she whacked the tiny god again. He screamed as he hit the wall. With each stroke of the paddle, Q's cries became weaker and weaker. Lwaxana was going to finish him off.

Deanna Troi burst into the court along with the *Enterprise* officers. "Mother, don't do this!"

"He has to say he's sorry," said Lwaxana. She held tiny Q in her hand, ready to smash him again.

"She couldn't really hurt me," Q squeaked.

"Stand aside, everyone," said Lwaxana. She swung her paddle back for the hardest smash yet.

"All right!" howled Q. "I'm sorry I did it!"

Lwaxana lowered the paddle. In a moment, Q was his usual size. He fell against a wall, gasping.

"You hurt me," Lwaxana said to him. "You think you are so much better than humans, so much above love. You know what? I think you're not good enough to feel love." She turned and walked away.

Q sat on the floor, trying to steady himself. "What are you looking at, Worf?" he grumbled.

"Nothing," said Worf happily. "I am looking at a great big nothing."

"That woman!" said Q, shaking with anger now. "No one has ever made me so mad. I can't stand her. I hate her as I have never hated anyone. I—"

"You will find, Q, that hate and love are often partners," said Picard.

"What are you talking about, Picard?" asked Q.

"You see, Q, the ones we love are the very ones who can make us the maddest."

"That's crazy." He frowned. "I couldn't be in love."

"Face it, Q," Picard told him. "You've been hanging around humans too long. You are starting to act just a little like us."

"Picard," said Q, "Get some hair. Your brain has caught a cold." With a flash of light, he disappeared.

Q reappeared atop the Nistral ship. He watched the *Enterprise* from a safe distance. "I must say," he sighed into empty space, "she was something!"

Lwaxana sat in her room looking in the mirror. She had the power of a goddess, but she couldn't even force a smile. Lwaxana Troi began to cry.

"Here," said a voice. A slim, blond man was standing in her room. He wore a plain green jumpsuit and held out a handkerchief.

Lwaxana was surprised. But she took the handkerchief and blew her nose. "Who are you?"

"Q," he said.

"That isn't funny. I know what Q looks like."

"Trust me on this. I'm Q, too."

"Q Two?" she said, confused.

"Whatever," said Q Two. "We've been keeping an eye on Q. We make sure he doesn't use his powers to cause trouble. When he tried to take your powers back again, I thought I'd teach him a lesson."

"You helped me keep the power?"

"Long enough for you to give Q a taste of his own medicine. You did quite a job. I took lots of pictures. I can't wait to show them to the others in the Q Continuum. I especially liked the business with the paddles."

Lwaxana started to smile. Then she laughed, a deep, lovely laugh. "It was clever, wasn't it? I made him think twice about hurting other people. He won't forget me!" she said.

"Got to take the powers back now," said Q Two. He snapped his fingers.

Lwaxana sagged slightly. She felt something disappear from within her, as if someone had turned off a light switch. She looked a little sad.

Then she brightened. "It's probably best this way," she said. "You seem wise, and I must say, you are rather goodlooking."

He put up a warning finger. "Don't even think it," he said, and he disappeared.

Lwaxana shook her head. "Can't blame a girl for trying," she said.

△ △ △

"So," Picard said, smiling, "I now pronounce you married."

Kerin and Sehra turned toward each other. Kerin took Sehra's face in his hands and kissed her. A cheer went up from all around. There was clapping, and there was a big sigh of relief. Picard closed the great book with a bang, and he gave silent thanks.